I0782108

# A GEORGIE & GIGI ADVENTURE

# The MARDI GRAS Mystery

George S. Corey ⚜ Art by CLEO

gistikidz™

New York

Cleo

For my grandmother,
the real Grand-mère Marie

# One

"TWEEEEEEEEEEEET" went the whistle, and the referee dropped a hockey puck between Georgie and a kiddo from the opposing team. Georgie and his BFF GiGi were co-captains of the second-grade hockey team at Our Lady Queen of Peace Elementary School in the suburbs of Washington, D.C.

Georgie was smart in class and was usually the first kid to get picked for team sports, except for basketball. He was fast but also short. He had black hair and wore a big smile—almost as big as the gap between his two front teeth.

GiGi's full name was Giselle after her grandmother,

who came from the French West Indies. She wore her hair in two pom-pom buns and was as good at sports as she was at anything creative. Georgie called her a "wonder girl."

Along with the rest of the team, the two G's had practiced very hard for the annual kiddos hockey championship.

It was thanks to their teacher and coach, Sister Elaine, that the championship game was being played at a very special place—the ice rink at the National Gallery of Art's Sculpture Garden in Washington, D.C.

Sister Elaine's "in" at the National Gallery was her famous friend, The Artist Cleo, who had met the kiddos a few months back when she gave a special Word Art presentation to the second graders at OLQP.

Georgie whacked the puck in GiGi's direction. She glided across the ice and drove the puck (or "biscuit," as she liked to call it) into the net—just as the buzzer sounded!

After their game-winning play, Georgie and GiGi's teammates gathered around them, cheering and high-fiving. Sister Elaine skated over to congratulate the entire team. "It's all about teamwork, kiddos," she told them, a big smile on her face.

As they all skated to the concessions area for juice and treats, Sister Elaine's cellphone rang. Her ring tone was Beyoncé's "Freedom," which the kiddos thought was pretty cool for a nun.

She answered the phone, chuckling, "You've got the coach of OLQP's hockey champions!"

"Elaine! I need you down in New Orleans right now!"

"Cleo, is that you? What's wrong?"

"Yes, it's me!" exclaimed Cleo, calling from her winter art studio in New Orleans. "Oh, Elaine, I'm so glad you picked up. We've got a Code Purple!"

"OMG, Cleo! It's really a Purple?!"

"Yes, I need your help. Please, hurry!"

Sister Elaine assured Cleo that she would not waste any time. After they hung up, Sister Elaine rushed over to Sister Mary Catherine, who was handing out little paper cups of apple juice.

"MC! MC! Cleo just called. There's a Code Purple in New Orleans!"

"There hasn't been a Code Purple in three years!" exclaimed Sister MC.

"What's a Code Purple?" asked Georgie, who along with GiGi had been listening to their teachers' worried conversation.

Sister Elaine pulled them into a quiet corner. She explained that a Code Purple is called any time Mardi Gras is in danger of being cancelled.

"What's Mardi Gras?" asked GiGi.

"*Mardi Gras* is French for Fat Tuesday, which is the day before Ash Wednesday," replied Sister Elaine.

"Oh, I know what Ash Wednesday is!" Georgie said excitedly. "It marks 40 days till Easter!"

"I *love* Easter," chimed in GiGi. "The Easter Bunny is tied with Santa Claus for my No.1 favorite."

Sister Elaine continued, "Fat Tuesday is only one day, but the Mardi Gras season is a *months*-long celebration of food, music, merriment, and fun. There are parades and dancing. Many people wear hats, wigs, masks, and even full costumes. The city of New Orleans is famous for its Mardi Gras festivities. But now ghosts have invaded one of the city's most well-known attractions, St. Louis Cathedral, scaring away tourists and partygoers.

"If Mardi Gras is cancelled, then Ash Wednesday is at risk of being cancelled. And if there's no Ash Wednesday, there's no Lent. And if there's no Lent—"

"There's no Easter, and no Easter Bunny!" blurted out GiGi.

"Exactly," sighed Sister Elaine. "So we need to get to the bottom of these ghosts and help Cleo save Mardi Gras before it's too late. This is not my first Code Purple, kiddos."

"Hopefully it will be the last," said Sister Mary Catherine, making the sign of the cross.

"MC, can I count on you to take care of my classes while I'm in New Orleans?" Sister Elaine asked her.

"Yes, of course, Sister," replied MC.

Sister Elaine turned to G and G. "Now, I'm going to need the help of my best junior sleuths. In Code Purples past, I've found that ghosts are often more responsive to kiddos than grownups. Can I count on you two to help me and Cleo solve this Mardi Gras mystery?"

Georgie and GiGi nodded enthusiastically. Not only did they want to help Sister Elaine and Cleo, but they also knew they'd be off from school!

"We'll be in the French Quarter, so it would be helpful to have a French speaker with us," Sister Elaine wondered aloud.

"I know just the person!" exclaimed Georgie.

# Two

Georgie's grandmother, Marie, arrived in her silver Porsche Cayenne with bright red leather seats. GiGi called them candy apple red, but Georgie insisted that they were fire engine red.

Marie was one cool granny, and she knew how to get things done. Both Georgie and GiGi called her Grandma Marie, or *Grand-mère* Marie in French, even though she was technically only Georgie's grandmother.

She was born and raised in Alexandria, Egypt, and now lived in Alexandria, Virginia—which she referred to as "coming full circle." She still possessed the athleticism that made her a star on the junior high and high school girls' basketball teams back in Egypt.

Sister Elaine considered Marie a friend, and was so happy that Georgie had come up with the idea of bringing her along. Grandma Marie was the perfect addition to their group of ghost detectives. Besides being fluent in French, she had witnessed a Code Purple herself when she was not much older than Georgie and GiGi. The French nuns at her school in Egypt were called to the rescue, just like Sister Elaine was being called now.

At that moment, as if by magic, a pink Prius emblazoned with a huge "Baked by Yael" symbol across the hood rolled up and Cleo's good friend Yael jumped out.

She was dressed in a panda suit, cute ears and all, carrying two white bakery boxes.

Yael was popular with the students at OLQP. She

made the best cake pops for birthday parties and school functions. She even baked gluten-free ones for the "celiac kiddos."

"Cleo called me right after she called you," Yael told Sister Elaine as they hugged hello. "I'm here to help, and I won't take no for an answer. Never underestimate the power of a panda suit."

Sister Elaine then introduced Yael to Marie, who said, "*Bonjour Yael! C'est la grande pâtissiere!*" She then translated what she said into English, "Hello Yael, the great cake maker!"

"That's me," Yael chuckled.

Sister Elaine pointed to the boxes. "I think I know what's inside those."

"Cake pops!" cried Georgie and GiGi.

"Well, yes," said Yael. "But not just regular cake pops. These are *magic* cake pops! The first box has little panda cake pops. Those will take you where you need to go."

"Like a magic skateboard?" asked Georgie.

"That lets you travel through time?" added GiGi.

Yael laughed. "I'm not *that good* a baker! No time travel, but these will get you to New Orleans and back."

"It's a heck of a lot easier than taking a plane," said Sister Elaine.

"And faster!" said Grandma Marie, smiling.

"What about the second box, Ms. Yael?" asked GiGi.

"I was in a rush to get here, so I just sprinkled the cake pops in the second box with generic all-purpose magic."

"How do they work?" asked Sister Elaine.

"You should know, Sister," cracked Yael. "Faith! You have to believe in what you're doing, truly believe, for the magic to work."

She then handed out panda pops to Georgie, GiGi, Sister Elaine, and Grandma Marie, and wished them luck.

They each unwrapped a cake pop and took a bite.

Suddenly, they were drawn into a magical tornado spout of spiraling, smiling panda faces.

Sister Elaine and Marie had their heads together the entire flight. Just like Georgie and GiGi. In no time, they gently landed. They were in New Orleans! And there was The Artist Cleo!

Cleo

CLEO

# Three

Georgie and GiGi raced to get to Cleo first and high-fived her. Then Georgie introduced his Grandma Marie to The Artist Cleo.

"*Ravie de vous rencontrer*," said Marie with a warm smile.

"Oh, you speak French!" Cleo replied. "Very nice to meet you, too. I've heard all about you from Elaine."

After a group embrace, Cleo stretched her arms out wide and announced, "Welcome to St. Louis Cemetery No.1, the oldest and most famous cemetery in New Orleans."

It felt a little spooky being in a cemetery at night,

but with three adults there, Georgie and GiGi didn't feel scared. And this was unlike any cemetery they'd ever seen.

"What are all these little houses?" asked GiGi.

"They're actually tombs," Cleo replied.

"Yes, children," interjected Sister Elaine, ever the teacher. "The tombs in this cemetery are above ground, and the 'little houses' are called mausoleums. The city of New Orleans is below sea level, and we wouldn't want caskets floating around, would we?"

Marie pulled a New Orleans guidebook out of her ginormous handbag, which could hold anything. "It says here that many famous people are buried in this cemetery."

"Oh, yes, there are many famous people who are resting here," Cleo told them. "One of the most popular sites is the tomb of Marie Laveau, the legendary Voodoo Queen of New Orleans.

"OOOOOOOOOH!" cried GiGi. "A Voodoo Queen."

"Sounds scary," said Georgie, wide-eyed.

"How scary can anyone named Marie be?" asked Grandma Marie.

Cleo laughed, saying, "Marie Laveau was hardly scary. In fact, she was a real woman of the people—one who wore many hats. She was a healer, a teacher, even a hairdresser at one point! She was what we'd refer to nowadays as a community leader and activist.

"Another famous gravesite belongs to Homer Plessy. He was part of the United States Supreme Court case *Plessy v. Ferguson*. That was a famous decision, but not a good one, because it basically said that discrimination was OK."

"Which it most certainly is not," chimed in Sister Elaine. "If my knowledge of history is correct, that Supreme Court ruling luckily was overturned by another case, *Brown v. Board of Education*."

"That's right," said Cleo. "Thurgood Marshall, one of the lawyers in that case, argued that no law could stop Black kids from attending the same school as white kids. Not only did Marshall win the case, but he went on to become the first Black man appointed to the Supreme Court."

"We met the first Black *woman* appointed to the Supreme Court!" exclaimed GiGi.

"You did?" asked Cleo.

"Ketanji Brown Jackson!" squealed GiGi.

"Indeed, they did," Sister Elaine said. "At our field trip to the Supreme Court Building, we were lucky enough to run into Justice Jackson. And she was kind enough to take some time out of her busy day to talk to our class."

"Best of all, she let us all have frozen yogurt from the *official* Supreme Court froyo machine," said Georgie.

Cleo then pointed out a pyramid-shaped tomb.

"Wow, who does that one belong to?" GiGi asked.

"You won't believe it, but that one's empty—so far,"

replied Cleo. "It belongs to the Hollywood actor Nicolas Cage, who is very much alive."

"He must've been a Boy Scout, like me," said Georgie. "Because our motto is *be prepared*." Everyone laughed.

Cleo invited them all back to her home for a quick snack before they got to sleuthing. As they exited the cemetery, Marie took each kiddo by the hand. Sister Elaine walked ahead of them alongside Cleo, who led them to a shiny new TrailMaster Taurus 6-Seater Golf Cart. It was the limousine of golf carts.

Sister Elaine put her hands on her hips. "This is what you're driving around in these days? What happened to your little convertible Mini Cooper?!"

"Oh, I made a trade with my favorite caddy at the New Orleans Country Club. He got the Mini and I got this tricked-out golf cart. Isn't it cool?"

"Super cool!" cried G and G.

"I heard about that club," said Marie. "It's supposed to have the best course in the city."

"Oh, do you play golf?" Cleo asked her.

"My grandma plays everything," Georgie said proudly. "Softball, basketball, video games, golf.

And she's good at everything, too."

Cleo was impressed. "Well," she said, addressing Marie and Elaine. "The three of us will have to hit the green some time *after* we take care of the ghosts. But first, let's go to my house!"

# Four

They bumped along in Cleo's golf cart until they crossed into the French Quarter, a special section of the city known as "the Crown Jewel of New Orleans." The wrought-iron balconies, hanging plants, and gas lanterns made Georgie and GiGi feel like they were in some magical place.

Cleo parked on the street in front of a beautiful complex of nine white stucco buildings surrounding a courtyard and pool. "This is where I live," she said, as she unlocked the front gate.

Before leading them into her house, she showed

them a very old-looking building that was different from the others. Grandma Marie read aloud from a brass plaque by the door. "*La Maison Hospitalière.*"

After translating the name into English—"the Hospitable House"—Cleo explained that the building they were standing in dated back to 1879, when it was a charitable home for poor Civil War widows.

"We're learning all about the Civil War in our history class, right Sister Elaine?" asked Georgie excitedly.

"That's right," nodded Sister Elaine.

GiGi jumped in, "We learned all about the Underground Railroad, and Sojourner Truth, and Harriet Tubman! Ms. Cleo, I bet you don't know what Harriet's nickname was."

"Tell me."

"Minty!" exclaimed GiGi.

"Well, you both must have a *very* good teacher," said Clco, giving Sister Elaine a quick wink.

"Oh, we do," Georgie said. "Sister is teaching us all about the presidents. Did you know that they call Abraham Lincoln 'Honest Abe,' and that Barack Obama's nickname when he was a kiddo was Barry?"

"And that the Teddy Bear is named after Theodore Roosevelt?" asked GiGi.

"I'm impressed," said Cleo. "You two sure do know a lot about the presidents."

"It's not just presidents," GiGi told her. "We're learning about all kinds of people from history, like Shirley Chisholm. She was the first Black woman elected to Congress and the first one to run for president!"

"And Fannie Lou Hamer," said Georgie. "She fought for civil rights and voting rights—"

"And women's rights!" cried GiGi.

"If you kiddos like history, and it sure sounds like you do," said Cleo. "You've come to the right place. New Orleans is full of history."

# Shirley Chisholm

# Fannie Lou Hamer

"There are ghosts everywhere in New Orleans!"

Cleo took out a big pitcher of lemonade and poured each of them a glass.

There was so much to see in Cleo's house. There was art everywhere. G and G fixated on four mannequin heads arranged on a table. Each wore a wild, colorful wig.

One was an electric blue upsweep with a glass on top. Another was a purple beehive style with Pippi Long-stocking braids and ribbons. There was a multicolored mohawk and a big pink bouffant with the motto. "The higher the hair, the closer to God."

"Those are my Mardi Gras wigs," Cleo told them. "Aren't they fun? Now, come on, let's get down to business—ghost business."

"You mentioned that you had a line on the ghosts," Sister Elaine said. "Shouldn't we be looking for them at St. Louis Cathedral?"

"Oh, we won't have to look for them," Cleo told her. "I've been, and they're definitely *there*. But I haven't been able to coax them into communicating with me. No one has."

"That's a problem," Marie said to herself. "Without communication, there can be no solution."

"Bingo," said Cleo. "I'm hoping that the ghosts around here can help broker talks with the ghosts haunting the cathedral."

"There are ghosts *here*?" Georgie asked, his voice trembling.

"Oh, sure," said Cleo. "There are ghosts everywhere in New Orleans!

"Most of the time, you don't really see them as much as feel their presence. But, don't worry, they seem friendly enough. The problem with the ghosts at St. Louis is that they're very visible and very loud. They're scaring away all the tourists who are here for Mardi Gras."

Georgie shook his head, saying, "And if there's no Mardi Gras, there's no Lent. And if there's no Lent, there's no Easter—"

"No Easter Bunny!" cried GiGi. "Sister Elaine explained everything to us."

"Let's just hope that you kiddos can get them to talk," Cleo said. "Ghosts tend to like kiddos a lot more than adults."

# Five

Cleo reached into her A-B-C-Dior Lady Di tote purse and pulled out two clear plastic devices about the size of iPhones and handed them to GiGi and Georgie.

Each one had a big orange button and a half-moon scale numbered 0-1-2-3-4-5 along the curve. The needle was set to "0."

Cleo told them the devices were called EMF Sensors and could detect electromagnetic fields.

She explained, "If the needle points to 5, and the sensor beep-beep-beeps like crazy, it means that electromagnetic fields have been detected. Translation: *Ghosts* have been detected!"

Georgie and GiGi immediately turned on the devices and started pointing them in every direction.

"What are electromagnetic fields anyway?" asked Georgie.

"Electromagnetic fields are like waves," said Sister Elaine.

"Like waves in the ocean?" asked GiGi.

"In a way, but you can't *see* these waves. They're invisible. They wiggle back and forth to form waves, and these waves make energy.

"And there are different kinds of waves. *Radio* waves make television and radio work. And *cellular* waves and Wi-Fi make cellphones and the internet work.

"Just like ocean waves, some are huge and some are small. Some are fast and powerful. And some are slow and weak."

"I bet things like X-ray machines and microwaves have fast and powerful waves," said Georgie.

"Yes, indeed!" exclaimed Sister Elaine. "Very good, Georgie."

So far, nothing. The needles on the EMF Sensors were stuck on "0."

"Cleo, where were you when you sensed the ghosts?" asked Marie. "What were you doing?"

"I was in my studio or in the garden, and sometimes by the pool. But, I was always painting or drawing."

"So, make art!" Sister Elaine cried. "That may draw out the ghosts."

Cleo pulled out a spiral-bound sketchbook and a sleeve of fat, pastel-colored chalk pieces. She turned to a fresh sheet of heavyweight paper and started sketching.

Georgie and GiGi stood on their tiptoes and peered over Cleo's shoulder to see what she was drawing. She was drawing *them*!

The pops in this box were shaped like fleur-de-lis, which means "flower of the lily" in French, a symbol of New Orleans' French heritage.

Minutes passed. Cleo put her chalk down. "This isn't working."

"Hey, I have an idea," said GiGi. "What about Yael's magic cake pops?"

"Yes, yes, yes!" shouted Georgie. "The second box!"

Grandma Marie produced the second box of cake pops from her bottomless handbag. The pops in this box were shaped like *fleur-de-lis*, which means "flower of the lily" in French, a symbol of New Orleans' French heritage.

They each picked up a cake pop that Yael had specially baked and sprinkled with generic all-purpose magic and took a big, delicious bite.

Suddenly, there was laughter. They looked up and three old-timey-looking men, all dressed in funny outfits, were floating above them. The ghosts had arrived.

# Six

Sister Elaine, Grandma Marie, and Cleo stepped in front of the children to shield them from the apparitions.

Mustering their courage, Georgie and GiGi stepped forward and bowed like an Old World lord and lady. The ghosts wore wide smiles and framed their faces with jazz hands. They were friendly ghosts!

"Hi! I'm GiGi, and this is my best friend, Georgie."

"And this is my Grandma Marie, Sister Elaine, and the famous artist Ms. Cleo!"

Two of the ghosts glided toward them. They were

dressed in monks' robes like Friar Tuck wore in *Robin Hood*, and each had a bald patch shaved on his head.

"*Bienvenue à la Nouvelle-Orléans*," the first one said before translating his greeting in a French-tinged accent. "Welcome to New Orleans!

"I am the ghost of Père Dagobert. I moved to this city from my native Quebec in 1722, and became a priest of the Parish of St. Louis in 1745."

"And I am the ghost of Antonio de Sedella, better known in these parts as Père Antoine," the other one said in a heavy Spanish accent. *Bienvenidos*, which means welcome."

Cleo whispered to Georgie and GiGi, "Père Antoine is quite famous, maybe the city's most famous priest of all time."

Père Antoine continued, "I was born in Málaga, Spain, in 1748, but made New Orleans my home in 1774. I proudly served as rector of St. Louis until my death in 1829."

"What's a rector?" asked Georgie.

"It means he was in charge of the cathedral," answered Sister Elaine. "He was the top banana of St. Louis Cathedral, like Principal Sister Theresa is at OLQP."

Again, Cleo excitedly whispered to G and G. "I've felt their presence but have never actually seen them till now! I told you kiddos, a lot of ghosts are much nicer to kiddos than us adults."

The third ghost made his presence known, tipping his feathered hat in a theatrical gesture. This one was definitely not a monk.

"Greetings!" he said, twirling his moustache. "Yes, I am he. The strapping swashbuckler, the bodacious buccaneer himself, 'The Ghost Pirate of New Orleans,' Reginald Hicks."

"Wow!" exclaimed Georgie. "You're a real pirate?"

"Well, I *was*. Yessiree. Fought for these United States in the Battle of 1812 under the command of privateer Jean Lafitte. Gave my life, I did."

Then, the ghost pirate produced three red roses out of thin air. He gently tossed them, one at a time, to Cleo, Grandma Marie, and Sister Elaine.

"Do you believe in *love*?" he asked rather dramatically.

Before any of them could reply he answered his own question, "I do! Even though you can't see love, or touch it, or smell it, or taste it, it is *real*."

"Like electromagnetic waves!" cried GiGi.

"I don't know what that means, but love-love-love is the realest thing in the world. It's what has kept me going all these years. Hundreds of years!

"Shortly before going off to war, I married a beautiful Creole woman. We became buccaneer and bride, we did, not a stone's throw from the cathedral.

"They call it Pirates Alley to this day, and I still wander those cobbled streets yonder, awaiting the fair ghost of my beloved to appear."

The ghost pirate suddenly took a businesslike tone. "Now, how may we be of service to you?"

"Well, sir, we have a Code Purple situation," replied Cleo.

"Not to worry, my child," said Père Antoine, reassuringly. "We have witnessed several Code Purples, as you call them, over the centuries."

"What about *our* Code Purple?" asked Sister Elaine. "Have you heard what's happening at St. Louis Cathedral?"

"*Oui!* Yes!" said Père Dagobert, "The ghosts, so many of them—47 to be precise—they are pestering the people and driving them away. Come, we will help you solve this little mystery, *eh?*"

"*Merci beaucoup*," said Grandma Marie, with a slight bow of her head. Then she turned to Georgie and GiGi. "That means thank you. Manners are manners, in any language."

Cleo

# Seven

They set out for the scenic 10-block walk to St. Louis Cathedral, with their three new ghostly friends floating above.

Georgie and GiGi waved their EMF detectors in every direction as they walked through the French Quarter.

"Those aren't party favors, kiddos!" Sister Elaine told them. "Now turn them off until we're inside the cathedral.

They passed Bourbon Street, then Royal Street. "Oh, this area is a very popular destination, known for its shops, restaurants, and art galleries," said Sister Elaine.

"How did you know that?" asked Cleo.

"What? A nun can't be on Instagram?"

Cleo laughed.

As they passed Chartres Street, Buccaneer Hicks pointed out his friend and commander Jean Lafitte's house.

"It was President James Madison who persuaded Jean and his pirate crew to come to the assistance of General Andrew Jackson in the Battle of New Orleans during the War of 1812," Hicks recalled with pride. "Our great victory in the battle stood as an important symbol to the British and to all of Europe of American majesty and might."

"Hey, you were pirate patriots!" exclaimed Georgie.

"I bet you can't say *that* five times, really fast?" teased GiGi.

"Bet I can!" Georgie raced out in one big breath. "Pirate patriot, pirate patriot, pirate patriot, pirate patriot . . . patriot . . . pirate . . . oh, no!"

As they came upon Barracks and Decatur Streets, Père Antoine and Père Dagobert pointed out their favorite jazz club.

"How do 300-year-old ghosts—men of the cloth no less—even know about jazz, let alone love it?" asked Sister Elaine.

Père Antoine replied, "What? 300-year-old ghosts can't be on Instagram?" They all laughed.

Cleo said that she, too, was a big fan of *le jazz*. She told them about the New Orleans Jazz & Heritage Festival and how the Jazz Museum, where she sat on the board of advisors, sponsored free jazz concerts every Tuesday. The art that Cleo created for the museum's annual gala called "Improvisations" even hangs in the museum!

Across the street from St. Louis Cathedral was the famous Café du Monde, known for its *beignets*—French doughnuts covered in powdered sugar.

Grandma Marie learned from her guidebook that

beignets and coffee have been served in that spot since the Civil War. She promised the kiddos that she would treat them to beignets and hot chocolate, but only *after* they took care of the ghosts.

"There's usually a long line outside Café du Monde that wraps around the block this time of year," said Cleo. "But the haunting of St. Louis has all but scared away visitors. Oh, we must save Mardi Gras before it's too late."

They were now at Jackson Square, a lush green park (with palm trees!) in front of the cathedral.

They looked up at the famous statue of General Andrew Jackson. He was on a horse waving his cap victoriously after winning the Battle of New Orleans.

Sister Elaine told them how Jackson rode his victory all the way to the White House, becoming the seventh president of the United States. Tens of thousands of people showed up to his inauguration party and they ate through a 1,400-pound wheel of cheese!

As they passed through the huge front doors of the cathedral, Grandma Marie took hold of Georgie and GiGi's hands. It felt spooky.

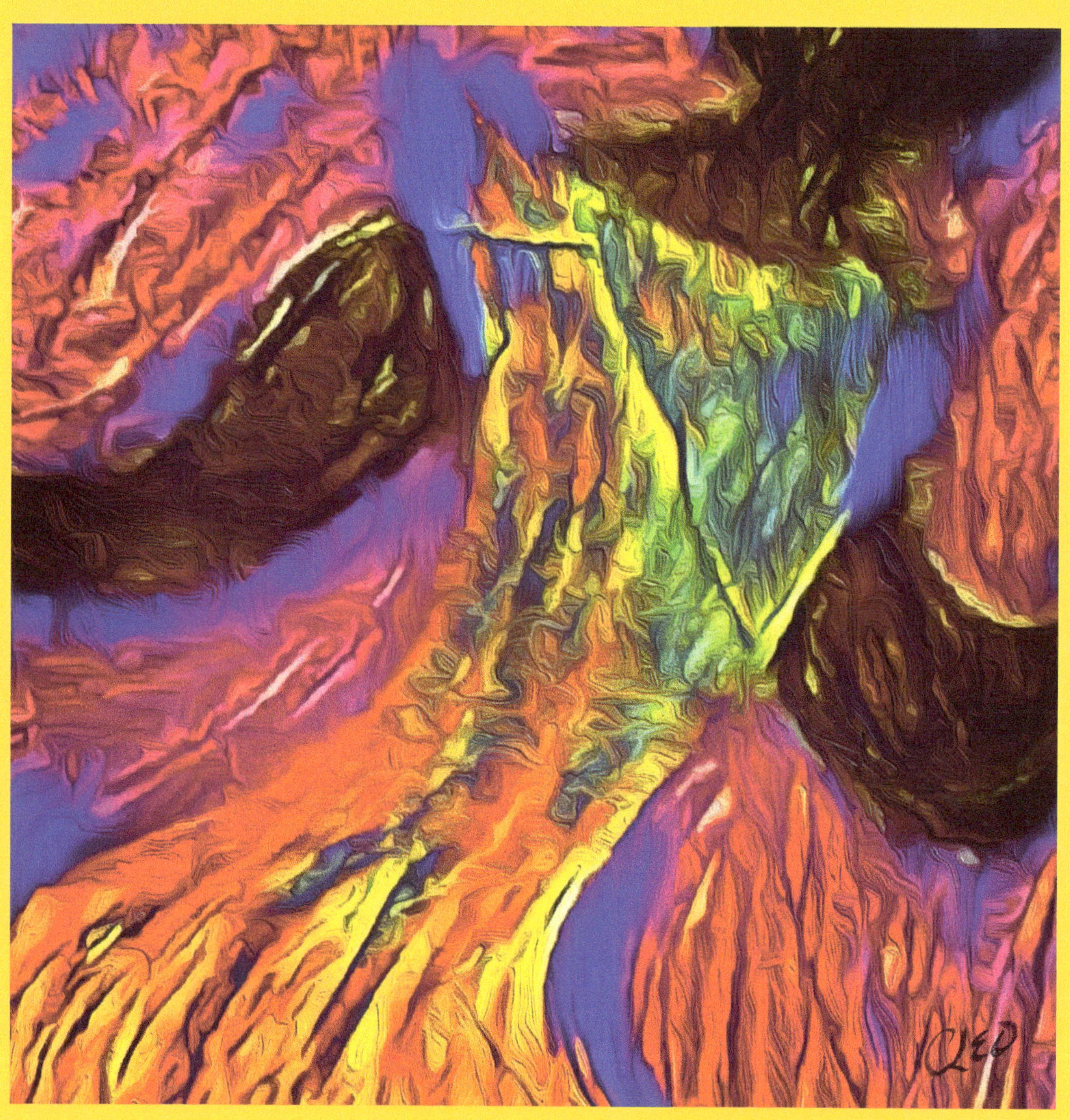

St. Louis Cathedral was old and majestic, with towering beams, enormous stained-glass windows and lots of marble, wood, and gold.

Their footsteps echoed. They all suddenly felt a chill. Georgie and GiGi pulled out their EMF Sensors, but there was no need. *The ghosts had arrived.*

Forty-six faintly transparent women swirled around them. They were all in formal ball gowns, laughing, singing, and chattering, louder and louder, until—

They quieted themselves and gathered around in a

half-circle as their Queen descended, making a grand entrance like Beyoncé atop a mirror-encrusted horse.

Her gown, jewels, and crown all shimmered, creating a haze of white light around her. She was beyond fancy. She was regal.

Père Antoine, Père Dagobert, and Buccaneer Hicks applauded, shouting "*Brava! Brava!*"

Cleo followed their lead, as did Sister Elaine, Grandma Marie, and Georgie and GiGi. Soon they were all clapping.

The dazzling ghost seemed satisfied, but not surprised, to receive such a reception. As if to reward them, she performed an elegant mid-air *pirouette.*

Georgie and GiGi stepped forward and bowed. This delighted the ghost queen, and she addressed them.

"Greetings, kiddos. You have no doubt come to see *me.* I am the ghost of Lady Germaine Cazenave Wells.

"I am the daughter of Count Arnaud Cazenave, who opened his restaurant Arnaud's in 1918. It was and has remained the finest restaurant in New Orleans, and in my opinion better than any restaurant in France and therefore the world.

"I am attended to by 46 ladies-in-waiting. But *I* am, have always been, and forever will be the most *beautiful*, most *fashionable* and—when I smile—the most *affable* ghost in all New Orleans.

"In my lifetime, I reigned as queen over 22 Mardi Gras balls, more than any other woman in the history of *Carnaval*. Even now, I am always gowned in one of my many, many, *many* Mardi Gras vestments."

Lady Germaine then stretched out her arms, saying, "Surely these *adults* have told you all about my namesake museum, the Germaine Cazenave Wells Mardi Gras Museum, housed in my father's restaurant.

"It is as extraordinary a place as the woman it's named for—*me*. The most exquisite gowns, masks, costume jewels, and many other mementos from days of Mardi Gras past are on display."

"Lady Germaine," said Cleo respectfully, taking her place between Georgie and GiGi. "Please allow me to introduce myself. I am The Artist Cleo."

"Ah, yes," nodded The Lady Germaine. "I have seen your work. You are quite talented."

"Thank you," Cleo continued. "As the Queen of Mardi Gras, won't you please consider taking up residence someplace else? Your haunting of St. Louis Cathedral in such dramatic fashion has scared people away from our city. Mardi Gras has been effectively cancelled."

Lady Germaine threw her head back in haughty laughter. "Why would I ever leave this lovely cathedral? It is the perfect setting for such finery to be shown off in an endless parade of Mardi Gras fashion. What else could I want or need? What could *you* possibly have to offer?"

"Psst, Cleo," Grandma Marie whispered. "I have an idea."

# Nine

The Code Purple team huddled in a corner of the cathedral as Père Antoine, Père Dagobert, and Buccaneer Hicks hovered above.

"So, tell us your idea, Marie," urged Sister Elaine.

"Tell us! Tell us!" cried G and G.

"Shhh," whispered Grandma Marie to the kiddos. "It was Cleo who gave me the idea."

"I did?" asked Cleo. "How?"

"Well, Lady Germaine and her ladies-in-waiting may have all these fancy tiaras, gowns, scepters, and jewels. But, what is the one thing they *don't* have?"

Then, Marie produced Cleo's big pink bouffant wig from her handbag.

"I had a feeling one of Cleo's wigs might come in handy, so I grabbed this one on the way out," confessed Grandma Marie with a naughty grin.

"What a terrific idea!" Cleo said. "It can't hurt to try, and it just may work."

The Code Purple team returned to find that Lady Germaine and the 46 spirits had started a kick-line and were now dancing the Can-Can.

They swooshed their petticoats left and right, kicking in unison.

"Lady Germaine, please come down," beckoned GiGi.

"We have a gift for you," said Georgie. "One that will make you even more beautiful."

Lady Germaine cut the music, then descended slowly and gave them a skeptical but curious look.

"What could possibly improve upon my beauty and the perfection of my costume?"

"*This*," said Cleo, presenting her with the big pink wig. "Who is 'The Queen of Mardi Gras' without her Mardi Gras *wig*?"

Lady Germaine brought her right hand to her mouth and gasped.

The spirit ladies swarmed around her. All of them were overwhelmed by the big wig that looked like a cloud of cotton candy.

"What about my ladies-in-waiting?" asked Lady Germaine. "Are we all to take turns wearing this one wig?"

"Of course not," said Cleo. "We can provide all of you with fancy wigs—*and* the fabulous shopping experience you deserve."

Lady Germaine raised an eyebrow. "What are your terms, Cleo?"

"All we ask is that you vacate the cathedral and allow Mardi Gras to continue in peace," replied Cleo. "In turn, I will take you to my personal wig makers at a remarkable shop called Fifi Mahony's. Every wig is custom-made by hand, so each is a one-of-a-kind work of art. They will make one for each of you."

After conferring with the other 46 spirits, Lady Germaine returned with her answer. "I accept. Now, take us to Fifi Mahony's!"

"Who is 'The Queen of Mardi Gras' without her Mardi Gras wig?"

# The
# Gallery
# of
# Magical
# Mardi Gras
# Wigs

Cleo

cleo

Cleo

# Ten

At Fifi Mahony's wig boutique, Lady Germaine was treated like royalty. Well, as the Queen of Mardi Gras, she *was* royalty.

In no time, she and her 46 ladies-in-waiting were fitted with the most extravagant, magnificent wigs they could have imagined.

To celebrate, Lady Germaine took them all—the 46 spirit ladies, the Code Purple team, Père Antoine, Père Dagobert, and Buccaneer Hicks—to her father's restaurant Arnaud's. They feasted on Seafood Gumbo, Soufflé Potatoes, and Mushrooms Véronique.

Georgie didn't think he even liked mushrooms until he tasted the Mushrooms Véronique at Arnaud's!

They made their way to the second floor, where a newly bewigged Lady Germaine gave them all a tour of the Germaine Cazenave Wells Mardi Gras Museum.

They oohed and aahed at the museum's holdings, which were both a history of and tribute to Mardi Gras. They especially enjoyed learning about the celebration's traditional colors—purple, green, and gold—and how they symbolized justice, faith, and power.

When they got outside, they couldn't believe their eyes. There were people everywhere! Mardi Gras was back in full swing! A parade made its way down the street led by a marching band blasting "When the Saints Go Marching In."

It came time to say goodbye to Lady Germaine and the ghostly ladies.

Georgie and GiGi asked her if they could call her

"Lady G" since they called each other "G" for short. Lady Germaine laughed and said, "Of course, children!"

Then she and her ladies-in-waiting blew them all kisses and vanished into thin air.

At Café du Monde, the kiddos had hot chocolate and the adults drank chicory coffee.

Georgie and GiGi finally got to eat the beignets they'd been promised. As they bit into the doughnuts covered in mounds of powdered sugar, their mouths were completely covered in white.

Père Antoine, Père Dagobert, and Buccaneer Hicks were floating above them all. The three ghosts decided to play a little trick on them.

They joined hands in a circle and spun around, faster and faster, causing the powdered sugar to spin into a mini cyclone. The snowy sugar was flying everywhere!

G and G could not stop giggling when they saw that Sister Elaine, Grandma Marie, and Cleo's faces had been covered in powdered sugar!

ater, after they said goodbye, or bid *adieu*, to The Artist Cleo and their new ghostly friends, Sister Elaine took out four of Yael's magical panda cake pops for Georgie, GiGi, Marie, and herself. They each took a bite, and once again were swept up into a swirling wind spout of panda faces.

Soon they found themselves back in Washington, D.C., seated in a pew at the Cathedral of St. Matthew the Apostle.

Sister Elaine looked around and told them in her church voice that it was Ash Wednesday. "You know what this means, kiddos, right? It worked! We saved Mardi Gras."

At recess the next day, Georgie and GiGi relived their ghostly adventures in New Orleans.

GiGi said her favorite part was when Cleo took them to Fifi Mahony's. Georgie said his favorite was when they went to Café du Monde, especially the powdered sugar cyclone!

They decided then and there that when they grew up, they would write a book about the Mardi Gras mystery. And they would ask The Artist Cleo to illustrate it!

When they returned to class, they told Sister Elaine about their idea to some day tell the story of their adventures in a book.

"Now *that's* a good idea. I hope I'm in it," she said with a wink.

*The "real-life" Marie, as a child, with her parents*
*Spirodon Saad and Adele Awaki Saad*

# Author's Note

Grandma Marie is based on my own real-life grandmother, Marie Saad Seraphim. Seraphim means "angel" and she was and still is our guardian angel. I called her Teta Marie (*teta* is Arabic for grandmother). I was her firstborn grandchild, and she was my best friend.

Teta would tell us stories about her childhood in Egypt and her days as a high school student at Notre Dame de Sion, where she got to know the future Queen of Egypt!

She would remind us that she was the best basketball player at Notre Dame de Sion and would beat her brothers at all sports. She never let us kids win at anything and always challenged us.

Even though she lived to 94, Teta always said she thought of herself as forever 16, never seeing herself as "old." And she was *fun*. She'd take us to restaurants ahead of Mama arriving so we could order french fries and onion rings, finishing everything quickly before Mama got there.

Teta never held back. In giving love, she did it completely. She would say she loved us like the heaven and the earth. She was a happy person, always. Being around her, you couldn't help but feel joy. Now, in the character of Georgie's Grandma Marie, we all get to be around her again and, hopefully, feel that same joy.

# Afterword

I am thrilled that these exciting adventures will continue. That's right, this is the *first* in a series of Georgie and GiGi books.

I created "G and G" as a way of teaching and entertaining my 14(!) nieces and nephews, and, now, my young readers. I have always believed that young people are as smart, as kind, and as thoughtful as grownups. And I have found them to be a lot more honest with themselves and each other. So that's why I love writing for kiddos—and kids and young adults, too!

The Artist Cleo sketched and painted all the art in this book as she has for all my books. In my book *Presidential Conversations for Kids*, or *PC4K*, Cleo created a super cool skateboard gallery. But I may love the art she created for this book *even more*. I hope you do, too! Cleo's amazing art—including colorful ghosts wearing big fancy wigs—makes this fun adventure even more fun!

I was so happy to tell a story set in one of my favorite cities, New Orleans, with my favorite young hero and heroine, Georgie and GiGi, and some of my favorite things: ghost detectors, magic cake pops, and spooky fun! The ghosts are *friendly* ghosts—that was important to me. They are the spirits of real and good people, including historical figures.

One of the most important themes of this story is how great teamwork can be. I wanted to show the kiddos being treated like equal team members by the adults—and by the ghosts! As Cleo always reminds me, we're better *together*.

With gratitude to all who made it possible, especially my readers,

*George S. Corey,*
Washington, D.C.

*Guess who?*

CLEO

# About the Author

**George S. Corey** is the author of the acclaimed books *Presidential Conversations* and *Presidential Conversations for Kids.* He is co-creator, along with The Artist Cleo, of the award-winning podcast *The Social Contract,* now in its fourth season. He lives in Washington, D.C., with his wife, Cynthia.

www.georgescorey.com

# About the Artist

**The Artist Cleo** is a celebrated visual artist who creates in multiple mediums. A frequent collaborator with George S. Corey, her socially conscious art can be seen in the books *Presidential Conversations* and *Presidential Conversations for Kids*. A former pupil of President Jimmy Carter, she is committed to inspiring and nurturing tomorrow's leaders.

www.theartistcleo.com

gistikidz™

*Get the gist!*